MR. MEN
TRIP TO THE MOON

Roger Hargreaves

Original concept by
Roger Hargreaves

Written and illustrated by
Adam Hargreaves

EGMONT

One day Mr Nonsense was reading the Nonsenseland Times when he had the idea of going to the moon.

"Well, if a cow can jump over it then it can't be too hard to get to," he announced to no one in particular.

Later that day he mentioned the idea to Mr Greedy.

Mr Greedy thought it was an excellent plan.

"I hear the moon's made of cheese," he said, licking his lips. "I like cheese."

But Mr Greedy did put Mr Nonsense straight about one thing.

"It's a very long, long way away."

So they went to see Mr Clever.

"What we need is a space rocket," explained Mr Clever. "A space rocket is something I've always wanted to build."

"Will that be very difficult?" asked Mr Nonsense.

"Well, it is rocket science, so the answer is yes," said Mr Clever, who rather likes to show off.

While Mr Clever built the rocket, the other two set about choosing fellow astronauts to travel with them.

Mr Nosey could not go because the space helmet would not fit over his nose.

Mr Tickle and Mr Tall could not go because neither of them could fit into the space suits!

And Little Miss Splendid refused to take off her hat which was no good at all.

Mr Clever had finished the rocket in record time, clever him, and the day of the launch arrived.

"Ten, nine, eight, seven, six, five, four, three, two, one, blast off!" cried Mr Clever, pressing the launch button.

But nothing happened.

Nothing happened because Mr Forgetful had forgotten to fill the fuel tank.

An hour later, the rocket took off, roaring up into the sky trailing a great cloud of smoke.

It rose higher and higher into the air, high above the earth, through the atmosphere and into outer space.

"Oh my!" cried Mr Worry. "I'm floating!"

And so he was.

And so was everyone else.

"We don't weigh so much in space," explained
Mr Clever, cleverly. "The air is much thinner up here."

"Unlike Mr Greedy," chipped in Mr Rude, rudely.

It wasn't long before Mr Greedy began to feel hungry, so he cooked spaghetti for everyone.

Perhaps not the most sensible idea!

When they arrived, Mr Nonsense was the first to walk on the moon because it had all been his idea.

Although, he kept an eye out for jumping cows.

It was Mr Worry who discovered strange footprints on the surface of the moon, which he followed; while worrying he was about to bump into a space alien.

He was rather relieved to find it was Little Miss Scary walking on her hands.

Mr Small could not believe it.

He could lift Mr Greedy above his head with one finger!

Everyone had a wonderful day on the moon.

Everyone except for Mr Greedy, who was disappointed to discover that the moon is not made of cheese.

"I told you so," said Mr Clever, something that Mr Clever never tires of saying.

The next day they packed up and went home.

It had been a splendid adventure and Mr Nonsense was very pleased with himself.

And so were all who lived in Nonsenseland.

All except one.

"Go to the moon? What nonsense."

Said the cow!

". . . cheese!"

When Little Miss Sunshine returned, Little Miss Magic turned her back into her old self. She then found Little Miss Bossy and Mr Rude and turned them back to normal as well.

Little Miss Dotty took a lot longer to find as she was hidden in a mouse hole, and being the dotty person that she is, she seemed not to have noticed that anything had happened.

"Are you feeling all right?" asked Little Miss Sunshine, after Little Miss Magic had said a few magic words.

"Why, of course I am," said Little Miss Dotty. "Why shouldn't I?"

"Oh, no reason," said Little Miss Sunshine, winking at Little Miss Magic.

"Although," said Little Miss Dotty, twitching her nose, "I really fancy a nice piece of . . ."

The Wicked Witch cat let out a screech and fled.

And, barking noisily, the Little Miss Sunshine dog set off in pursuit and chased the Wicked Witch cat far away. So far away that she would never find her way back.

It was then that Little Miss Magic turned the Wicked Witch into a cat!

A smelly, scraggy, black cat.

A smelly, scraggy, black cat that suddenly found herself looking up at a scary yellow dog.

The next day, at sunrise, Little Miss Sunshine and

Little Miss Magic knocked at the Wicked Witch's door.

The Wicked Witch opened it and with a flash,

her spell turned Little Miss Sunshine into a dog.

"Hee, hee, hee," cackled the Wicked Witch. "That worked like a dream."

"There's a Wicked Witch living in Whispering Wood," explained Little Miss Sunshine, breathlessly, when she arrived. She then told Little Miss Magic what she had seen and more importantly what she had heard.

". . . and I'm going to be turned into a dog tomorrow morning!" she gasped.

"That's awful!" said Little Miss Magic. "But this is just the sort of problem that I like dealing with."

"I hoped you would say that," said Little Miss Sunshine.

"Now, I'll tell you what we are going to do . . ." continued Little Miss Magic.

She tip-toed round to the front door where the Wicked Witch had left her broomstick leaning against the wall. And without thinking whether she could fly a broomstick or not, Little Miss Sunshine hopped on.

As it turned out she could. Just about. The broomstick rose up into the air with a wobbly Little Miss Sunshine perched on top.

Little Miss Sunshine knew exactly who would be able to help - Little Miss Magic. The broomstick took her to Little Miss Magic's house in no time at all.

And this is what she heard:

"Hubble, bubble,
Toil and trouble,
Eye of newt and hair of hog,
Early tomorrow morning,
Turn Little Miss Sunshine into a dog!"

Little Miss Sunshine realised that she needed help and she needed it fast.

Nervously, Little Miss Sunshine crept up to the window and cautiously peered in.

The Wicked Witch was standing beside a large, black cauldron hanging over a fire. She was muttering to herself as she stirred revolting ingredients into the steaming pot. Little Miss Sunshine listened hard to hear what she was saying.

Suddenly, with a rustle of leaves, a Witch flew out from behind a tree.

A Wicked Witch on a broomstick!

A horrible hook-nosed, hairy, warty Wicked Witch, dressed in black.

Little Miss Sunshine felt very afraid, but she bravely decided to follow the Wicked Witch into Whispering Wood. It didn't take Little Miss Sunshine long to find the Wicked Witch's ramshackle cottage.

Little Miss Dotty had turned into a mouse!

A very confused, dotty, blond-haired mouse.

When Little Miss Sunshine heard the same laugh she had heard the two days before, she ducked behind a bush and waited to see if she could find out who it came from.

On her walk the following day, Little Miss Sunshine had nearly caught up with Little Miss Dotty when there was another blinding flash.

But at that moment there was a bright flash. And when Little Miss Sunshine reached where Mr Rude had been standing, she discovered that he had turned into a toad.

A red, very rude, angry looking toad.

And just like the day before, Little Miss Sunshine heard a cackling laugh. But this time it seemed to be coming from a nearby tree.

The next day was much nicer. The sun was out and there was not a cloud in sight. Little Miss Sunshine was happily walking along, wondering what had happened to Little Miss Bossy, when she saw Mr Rude walking towards her.

"I will be nice to Mr Rude," thought Little Miss Sunshine, "or he will be rude to me."

However, as she got closer, the most incredible thing happened. There was a bright flash and Little Miss Bossy turned into a bat!

A blue, very squeaky, bossy sort of a bat.

"How extraordinary!" exclaimed Little Miss Sunshine, as she watched Little Miss Bossy flap her wings and fly away.

But almost as extraordinary, was the cackling laugh Little Miss Sunshine thought she heard coming from the clouds above.

Little Miss Sunshine was going for a walk.

The weather was not very nice, but it takes a lot more than a bit of rain to dampen Little Miss Sunshine's spirits.

In the distance, she saw Little Miss Bossy approaching.

"I will be nice to Little Miss Bossy," thought Little Miss Sunshine, "so she won't boss me around."

LITTLE MISS SUNSHINE
and the Wicked Witch

Roger Hargreaves

Original concept by
Roger Hargreaves

Written and illustrated by
Adam Hargreaves

EGMONT